W9-BVR-412

KAY THOMPSON'S ELOISE

Eloise Has a Lesson

STORY BY **Margaret McNamara**

ILLUSTRATED BY **Kathryn Mitter**

Ready-to-Read

Simon Spotlight
New York   London   Toronto   Sydney   New Delhi

SIMON SPOTLIGHT

An imprint of Simon & Schuster Children's Publishing Division

1230 Avenue of the Americas

New York, NY 10020

First Simon Spotlight hardcover edition July 2018

First Aladdin Paperbacks edition January 2005

For information about special discounts for bulk purchases, please contact Simon & Schuster

Special Sales at 1-866-506-1949 or business@simonandschuster.com.

The text of this book was set in Century Old Style.

Manufactured in the United States of America 0618 LAK

2 4 6 8 10 9 7 5 3 1

The Library of Congress has cataloged a previous edition as follows:

Library of Congress Cataloging-in-Publication Data

McNamara, Margaret.

Eloise has a lesson / written by Margaret McNamara ;

illustrated by Kathryn Mitter.—1st ed.

p. cm.—(Ready-to-read) (Kay Thompson's Eloise)

Summary: Eloise would rather tease her tutor,

Philip, than let him teach her math.

[1. Teachers—Fiction. 2. Teasing—Fiction. 3. Arithmetic—Fiction.]

I. Mitter, Kathy, ill. II. Title. III. Series. IV. Series: Kay Thompson's Eloise.

PZ7.M47879343En 2005

[E]—dc22

2004009343

ISBN 978-1-5344-1509-6 (hc)

ISBN 978-0-689-87367-6 (pbk)

I am Eloise.
I am six.

I am a city child.

I live in a hotel
on the tippy-top floor.

This is Philip.

He is my tutor.
He is no fun.

Here is what I do not like:
doing math
for one half hour
in the morning.

Here is what I like:
teasing Philip.

Philip says, "Hello, Eloise."

I say, "Hello, Eloise."

Philip says, "Math time."

I say, "Bath time?"

Philip says, "Eloise, please."

I say, "Eloise, please."

Philip says,
"What is five plus six?"

I say, "You do not know?"

"Nanny!" says Philip.
"Make Eloise behave."
"Eloise, behave," says Nanny.

Chalk makes a very good straw.

"What is five plus six?"
says Philip.

"Five plus six is the same as
six plus five," I say.

Philip says, "Oh, Eloise."

I say, "Oh, Eloise."

Nanny says,
"Math time is nearly over.

"Time to finish up, up, up."

Philip says, "Eloise."

I say, "Philip."

Philip says, "Think."

I say, "I am thinking."

Philip says,
"What is five plus six?"

"It is eleven," I say.
"And the lesson is over."

Ooooooooo,
I absolutely love math.